Fireman Sam
AND THE FLOOD

by Alison Boyle
Illustrations by The County Studio

HEINEMANN · LONDON

"At last," Bella sighed as she closed the cafe one evening.
"Rosa, you stay here while I run my bath."

But as soon as Bella had gone, Rosa went too!

Upstairs, Bella turned on the bath taps. "When I've given Rosa her milk, the bath should be full," she thought.

Bella came out onto the landing and looked down the stairs.
"Rosa! Rosa!" she called, but Rosa had gone.

"R O S A !" Bella shouted, going out into the garden, but there was no sign of the cat.

Bella looked along the path and in the vegetable patch.
"Rosa," she called. "Here, puss, puss, puss."

She looked under the hedge. But there was no sign of Rosa.

Then Bella saw Trevor Evans on his way home in his bus.
"Can I help you?" he asked.

Fireman Sam came past on his way home.
"Anything the matter?" he called.

Soon everyone in Pontypandy was out looking for Rosa. But there was no sign of her.

"Let's stop for a rest," said Bella. "Who would like a hot drink and some biscuits?"

Everyone went into the cafe with Bella. The first thing Bella saw when she turned round was Rosa!

The next thing she saw was water dripping through the ceiling.

"Call the Fire Brigade!" shouted Fireman Elvis Cridlington.
"Oh! We're here already!"

It was quite dark in the cafe. Bella went to turn on the lights.

"Don't!" said Fireman Sam. "You must not touch anything electric. It's very dangerous."

"If the wires are wet, you might get an electric shock. We must find out where the water is coming from."

"We can use our torches," said Elvis, switching his on.
"Good idea," said Fireman Sam. "Come on. We must go
upstairs."

The firemen ran upstairs. "Oh dear," said Fireman Sam.
"Bella forgot to turn off the bath taps."

Elvis turned off the taps. Fireman Sam pulled out the bath plug to let the water drain away.

Down in the cafe everyone helped to mop up the water.
"Don't use the electricity until it has been checked,"
said Fireman Sam.

"I won't," promised Bella. "I think it's time for a drink of milk and some biscuits, don't you, Rosa?"

Rosa just purred.